This Walker book
belongs to:

_____

_____

_____

B.S.U.C. - LIBRARY

00319682

For Jasmine

First published 1993 by Walker Books Ltd
87 Vauxhall Walk, London SE11 5HJ

This edition published 2007

10 9 8 7 6 5 4 3 2

Text © 1993 Vivian French
Illustrations © 1993 John Prater

The moral rights of the author and illustrator
have been asserted.

This book has been typeset in Garamond.

Printed in China

All rights reserved

British Library Cataloguing in Publication Data:
a catalogue record for this book
is available from the British Library.

ISBN 978-1-4063-0633-0

www.walkerbooks.co.uk

BATH SPA UNIVERSITY
NEWTON PARK LIBRARY

Class No.
JF4 FRE

Coutts   28/10/09

Once Upon a Time

Conceived and illustrated by John Prater
Text by Vivian French

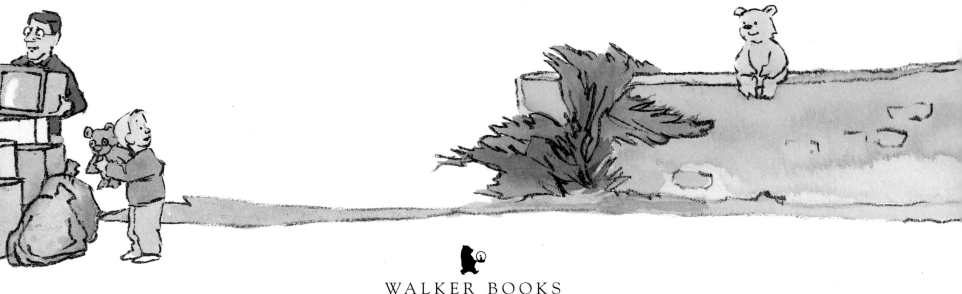

WALKER BOOKS
AND SUBSIDIARIES
LONDON · BOSTON · SYDNEY · AUCKLAND

Early in the morning
Cat and me.
Not much to do.
Not much to see.

Dad's off to work now
Mum's up too.
Not much to see.
Not much to do.

Day's getting older
Sun's up high.
Wave to a little girl
Hurrying by.

Mum's cleaning windows.
Here's a bear
Making a fuss
About a chair.

Ride my tricycle
For a while.
There's an egg
With a happy smile.

Mum's in the garden.
Washing's dry.
Why do babies
Always cry?

We've got sandwiches –
Cheese today.
Why's that wolf saying
"Come this way"?

I like jumping
To and fro.
That wolf's howling
He's hurt his toe.

Mum's drinking coffee.
We can chat.
I tell her my jump
Is as big as THAT!

Here's Dad home again!
Time for tea.
I wave to him
And he waves to me.

Dad's washing dishes.
I look out.
Did I hear someone
Walking about?

Time for my story.
I yawn and say,
"Nothing much happened
Round here today."

Another title by
John Prater

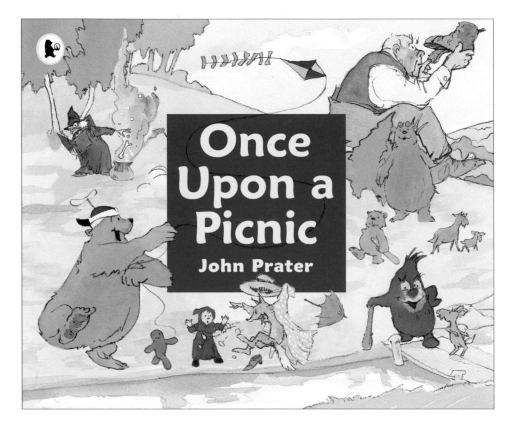

ISBN 978-1-4063-0632-3

Available from all good bookstores

www.walkerbooks.co.uk